# Trying Tricks

Story by Geoff Alan
Illustrated by Alan Willow

Based on a Martin Gates Production © 1996 BMG Entertainment,
Licensed by Just Licensing Limited. All rights reserved.
Published in Great Britain in 1997 by World International Ltd.,
Deanway Technology Centre, Wilmslow Road, Handforth, Cheshire SK9 3FB.
Printed in Finland. ISBN 0 7498 2856 0

One morning, Rat, Mole and Badger each received a letter from Toad, asking them to visit him urgently.

Puzzled, they hurried to Toad Hall.

Badger led the way to the front door. When he stepped onto a new doormat, it let out a shrill "SQUEAK!"

SQUEAK!

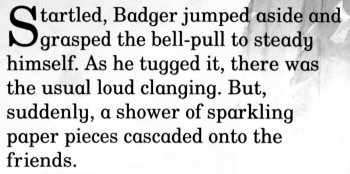

Startled, Badger jumped aside and grasped the bell-pull to steady himself. As he tugged it, there was the usual loud clanging. But, suddenly, a shower of sparkling paper pieces cascaded onto the friends.

Next moment, all three stared in astonishment at a funny face that peered around the door.

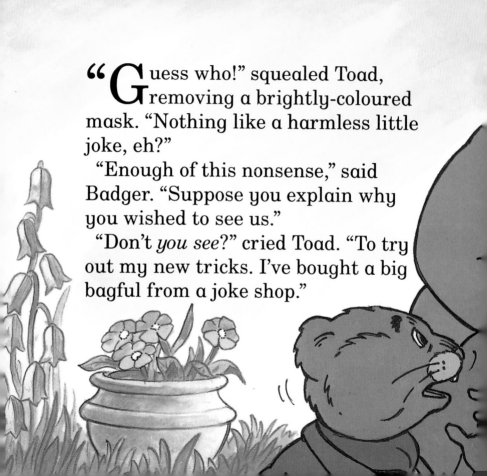

"**G**uess who!" squealed Toad, removing a brightly-coloured mask. "Nothing like a harmless little joke, eh?"

"Enough of this nonsense," said Badger. "Suppose you explain why you wished to see us."

"Don't *you see*?" cried Toad. "To try out my new tricks. I've bought a big bagful from a joke shop."

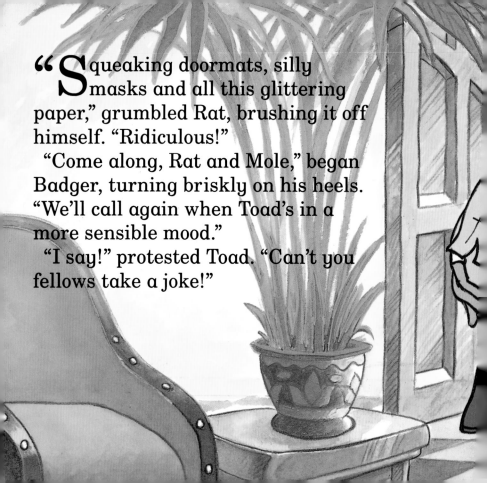

"Squeaking doormats, silly masks and all this glittering paper," grumbled Rat, brushing it off himself. "Ridiculous!"

"Come along, Rat and Mole," began Badger, turning briskly on his heels. "We'll call again when Toad's in a more sensible mood."

"I say!" protested Toad. "Can't you fellows take a joke!"

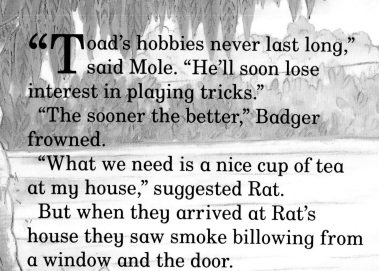

"**T**oad's hobbies never last long," said Mole. "He'll soon lose interest in playing tricks."

"The sooner the better," Badger frowned.

"What we need is a nice cup of tea at my house," suggested Rat.

But when they arrived at Rat's house they saw smoke billowing from a window and the door.

Rat quickly snatched up a bucket from his shed nearby. He filled it with river water and rushed inside the house. The others followed to find no fire but a second rat standing over the stove.

"Surprise!" called the visitor, cheerily.

"Monty!" cried Rat. "What are you doing here?"

As the smoke cleared, Rat saw dirty pots and pans everywhere. A glass of milk lay spilt on the floor and everything had been tipped out of the larder.

"Just burning, I mean, cooking a snack as you weren't around to do it for me, Ratty," added Monty. "I overdid a sausage and some toast!"

The newcomer was wearing Rat's best blazer. He had dropped butter down the front.

"I've come to spend the summer with you, Ratty," said Monty. "I know you'll be pleased! Oh, I've borrowed some clothes of yours, too."

"Monty's a distant cousin," Rat gloomily told Badger and Mole.

$M$onty waved carelessly, knocking over a bag of flour. "Oops! Nothing you can't clear up, Ratty," he said. "I must try your boat later!"

While Monty ate hungrily, a grim-faced Rat took his friends outside.

"I'll get no peace till he's gone," he whispered. "What am I to do?"

"Nothing," replied Badger, mysteriously. "We'll leave that to Toad!"

Before long, Badger and Mole returned with Toad.

"My dear fellow," beamed Toad, holding out a gloved hand to greet Monty.

As Rat's cousin went to shake hands, Toad's glove blew up like a balloon then flew into the air.

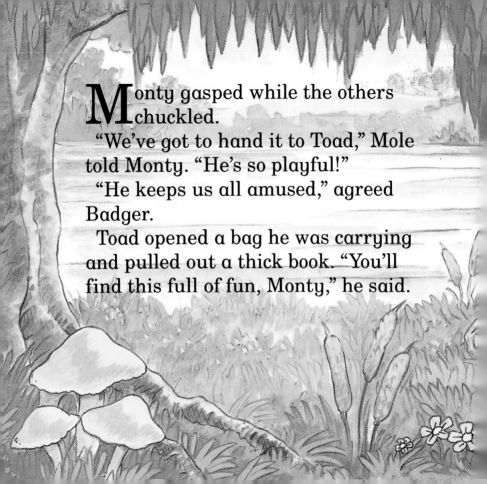

Monty gasped while the others chuckled.

"We've got to hand it to Toad," Mole told Monty. "He's so playful!"

"He keeps us all amused," agreed Badger.

Toad opened a bag he was carrying and pulled out a thick book. "You'll find this full of fun, Monty," he said.

Toad opened the book and a huge, wriggly toy worm sprang out at Monty. With a yell, he collapsed into a chair.

"There! What could be funnier!" cried Toad.

"Toad visits all the time," grinned Rat. "It's such a treat."

"Talking of treats," cried Toad, "I've brought lemonade and a sponge cake."

Toad took them from his bag. He poured the lemonade into plastic cups. But Monty's leaked all over him.

"What a laugh! Have some sponge," giggled Toad, offering it to Monty.

But the cake jumped off the plate into his lap, then bounced across the floor.

"It's sponge rubber!" squealed Toad.

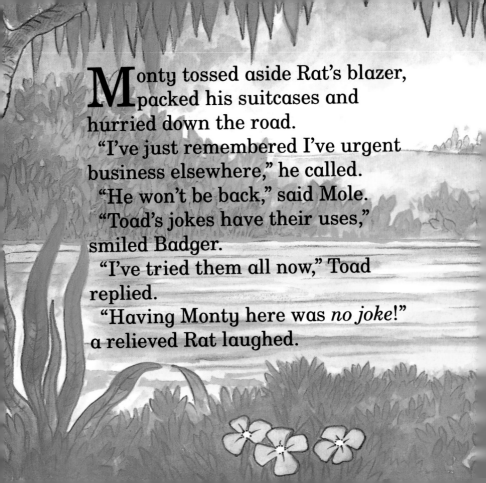

Monty tossed aside Rat's blazer, packed his suitcases and hurried down the road.

"I've just remembered I've urgent business elsewhere," he called.

"He won't be back," said Mole.

"Toad's jokes have their uses," smiled Badger.

"I've tried them all now," Toad replied.

"Having Monty here was *no joke*!" a relieved Rat laughed.

## Special offer to our Wind In The Willows readers.

n every Wind In The Willows book produced by World International Ltd., you
will find a special token. Collect six tokens and we will send you a super
ng size poster featuring all The Wind In The Willows characters.

eturn this page together with your six tokens to:-

arketing Dept, WITW, World International Ltd, Deanway Technology Centre,
Wilmslow Road, Handforth, Cheshire, SK9 3FB

our Name _____ Age _____

ddress _____

_____

_____

_____ Postcode _____

gnature of Parent/Guardian _____

nclose six tokens - please send me a Wind In The Willows poster.

may occasionally wish to advise you of other Wind In The Willows gifts. ☐
u would rather we didn't please tick this box.

Offer open to residents of UK, Channel Isles and Ireland only.

Collect six of these tokens
You will find one inside every
Wind in the Willows book which
has this special offer.

**1 TOKEN**

Titles in

If you have any difficulty obtaining any of these books, please contact the
Marketing Department at:
World International Limited, Deanway Technology Centre,
Wilmslow Road, Handforth, Cheshire SK9 3FB
Telephone: 01625 650011